BY
SCOTT SONNEBORN

ILLUSTRATED BY
OMAR LOZANO

THE
NORTH
POLICE

Computer Meltdown

The North Police is published by
Picture Window Books
a Capstone Imprint
1710 Roe Crest Drive
North Mankato, Minnesota 56003
www.capstonepub.com

Cataloging-in-Publication Data is available at the Library of Congress website.
ISBN: 978-1-4795-6485-9 (library binding)
ISBN: 978-1-4747-0032-0 (paperback)
ISBN: 978-1-4795-8476-5 (eBook)

Summary: Somebody stole Santa's computer! Without his lists, how will he know
where to deliver presents? If the North Police's greatest detectives can catch the
criminal, they'll have another name for Santa's naughty list!

Designer: Bob Lentz

Printed in China by Nordica
0415/CA21500537
042015   008843NORDF15

TABLE OF CONTENTS

(NORTH POHL-eess)

The North Police are

the elves who solve crimes

at the North Pole.

These are their stories . . .

CHAPTER 1
Santa's Computer

Inside Santa's workshop
was a computer. Every day,
Santa sat at this computer.
Every day, he added names to
his naughty and nice lists.

But not today . . .

Santa's computer was missing!

"It was here yesterday," Santa told the North Police's two greatest detectives. "Now there's just a puddle."

"Christmas is tomorrow," said Santa sadly. "How will I know who should get presents without my lists? You've got to find out what happened to my computer!"

 "Maybe the computer had a meltdown," said Detective Sprinkles. "It is rather warm in here."

"I've never heard of a computer melting into water," said Detective Sugarplum. "But there's one way to find out if that's what happened."

"To the lab!" Sprinkles said.

The North Police placed
the water in a small baggy.

"To all a good night crime
solving!" exclaimed Santa as
the North Police left.

CHAPTER 2
The North
Police Lab

At the lab, Sprinkles and

Sugarplum waited. Their lil'

helper elf tested the water.

First, he poured the water

into a test tube. Then he put

it under a microscope.

A minute later, the lil'
helper took off his safety
goggles and read the results.

"This is water," he said.

"Computer water?" asked
Detective Sprinkles.

"No, water water," the elf

explained. "Melted snow."

The lil' helper lifted the

test tube to his mouth. He

drank every last drop.

"Melted snow!" shouted Detective Sugarplum. "Let's take another look at the crime scene, Sprinkles. I might know what happened to Santa's computer!"

CHAPTER 3
Cold Case

The two North Police detectives returned to the scene of the crime.

"Look," said Sugarplum, pointing at the floor. "There's more water over here."

"So?" replied Sprinkles. "It's just melted snow."

"Exactly!" said Detective Sugarplum. "And look where it leads . . ."

The puddles of water led

right to the bathrooms.

There were three

bathrooms: the Women's

Room, the Men's Room, and

the Snowmen's Room.

WHAM! WHAM! Detective
Sugarplum knocked on the
door to the Snowmen's Room.

"Open up!" she said. "It's
the North Police!"

There was no answer.

"If there's a snowman in there, button up your coal buttons," said Sugarplum. "We're coming in!"

The two elves burst into

the Snowmen's Room.

"Brrr," said Sprinkles.

"This isn't like any other

bathroom I've ever seen."

"That's because you're not a snowman," said a voice.

The two North Police detectives turned and saw a snowman. He was holding Santa's computer!

"How did you know I took

it?" asked the snowman.

"The melted snow," said

Detective Sugarplum. "That's

what gave you away."

The snowman nodded.

"It was so hot in Santa's Workshop that I started to melt," the snowman said. "So I grabbed the computer and brought it here."

"I knew taking the computer was wrong, but I did it anyway," the snowman said. "I just had to know if my name was on Santa's list!"

"Well, you're definitely on Santa's list now," said Detective Sprinkles.

"Really?" asked the snowman. "Naughty or nice?"

Sugarplum handcuffed the snowman. "I'll let you figure that out," she said.

The North Police smiled.

"Another case neatly wrapped!" they cheered.

CASE CLOSED!

6' 6"
6' 0"
5' 6"
5' 0"
4' 6"
4' 0"
3' 6"
3' 0"

CASE 001   NORTH POLICE
CLANCY
Snowman • Height 6'0" • Weight 250

GLOSSARY

clue (KLOO) — something that helps you find an answer to a question or mystery

detective (di-TEK-tiv) — one who investigates crimes

microscope (MYE-kruh-skope) — an instrument with powerful lenses used to make small things appear larger

naughty (NAW-tee) — badly behaved or not following rules

test tube (TEST TOOB) — a glass tube that is closed at one end and used in lab experiments

These are their stories . . .

only from

PICTURE WINDOW BOOKS!

AUTHOR

Scott Sonneborn has written dozens of books, one circus (for Ringling Bros. Barnum & Bailey), and a bunch of TV shows. He's been nominated for one Emmy and spent three very cool years working at DC Comics. He lives in Los Angeles with his wife and their two sons.

ILLUSTRATOR

Omar Lozano lives in Monterrey, Mexico. He has always been crazy for illustration, constantly on the lookout for awesome things to draw. In his free time, he watches lots of movies, reads fantasy and sci-fi books, and draws! Omar has worked for Marvel, DC, IDW, Capstone, and more.